# The Story of Doctor Dolittle

Hugh Lofting

Condensed and Adapted by
KATHRYN KNIGHT

Illustrated by
NICK PRICE

Cover Illustrated by
LAURA FERNANDEZ
RICK JACOBSON

Dalmatian Press

The Junior Classics have been
adapted and illustrated with care and thought
to introduce you to a world of famous authors, characters, ideas,
and great stories that have been loved for generations.

Editor — Kathryn Knight
Creative Director — Gina Rhodes-Haynes
And the entire classics project team
of Dalmatian Publishing Group

THE STORY OF DOCTOR DOLITTLE

Printed in the United States of America

# FOREWORD

*A note to the reader—*

A classic story rests in your hands. The characters are famous. The tale is timeless.

This Junior Classic edition of *The Story of Doctor Dolittle* has been carefully condensed and adapted from the original version (which you really *must* read when you're ready for every detail). We kept the well-known phrases for you. We kept Hugh Lofting's style. And we kept the important imagery and heart of the tale.

Literature is terrific fun! It encourages you to think. It helps you dream. It is full of heroes and villains, suspense and humor, adventure and wonder, and new ideas. It introduces you to writers who reach out across time to say: "Do you want to hear a story I wrote?"

Curl up and enjoy.

# CONTENTS

# CHARACTERS

DOCTOR JOHN DOLITTLE — the kind and clever animal doctor from Puddleby-on-the-Marsh

SARAH DOLITTLE — the Doctor's sister

MATTHEW MUGG — the catfood man

AFRICAN KING AND QUEEN — rulers of the Jolliginki

PRINCE BUMPO — the young African prince with dreams of heroic adventures

POLYNESIA THE PARROT — the Doctor's teacher

CROCODILE — who lives (in peace) in the Doctor's fishpond

CHEE-CHEE THE MONKEY — who knows Africa

JIP THE DOG — who can sniff out anything!

DAB-DAB THE DUCK — who is friendly and helpful

GUB-GUB THE BABY PIG — who tends to fret and cry

TOO-TOO THE OWL — who has very sharp ears

# CHARACTERS

SWALLOW — the messenger who leads to Africa

WHITE MOUSE — the "stow-away" aboard
the ship

PUSHMI-PULLYU — (Push-me Pull-you) a very
rare, polite animal with two heads and no tail

Animals who help the Good Doctor
    PORPOISES — who bring wild onions
    LIONS, ZEBRAS, GIRAFFES — help nurse
    the sick
    MONKEYS AND GORILLAS AND
    ORANGUTANS AND BABOONS AND
    CHIMPANZEES — hold a council to reward
    the Doctor
    SWALLOWS — who pull the ship
    RATS — who warn that the ship is sinking
    EAGLES — who search for the boy's uncle
    SHARKS — who help the pirates decide…

BEN ALI — the mean pirate, the Dragon of Barbary

LITTLE BOY — a sad little lad found on the
pirates' ship who is missing his uncle

BOY'S UNCLE, THE FISHERMAN — saved by
Jip and a can of mints

# The Story of
# Doctor Dolittle

# CHAPTER ONE

# Puddleby

Once upon a time, many years ago—when our grandfathers were little children—there was a doctor, and his name was Dolittle. John Dolittle, M.D. "M.D." means that he was a real doctor and knew a whole lot.

He lived in a little town called Puddleby-on-the-Marsh. All the folks, young and old, knew him well. Whenever he walked down the street in his high hat everyone would say, "There goes the Doctor! He's a clever man." And the dogs and the children would all run up and follow behind him. Even the crows that lived in the church tower would caw and nod their heads.

# THE STORY OF
# DOCTOR DOLITTLE

The house he lived in was quite small, but his garden was very large. It had stone seats and weeping willow trees hanging over. His sister, Sarah Dolittle, was housekeeper for him, but the Doctor looked after the garden himself.

He was very fond of animals and kept many kinds of pets. He had goldfish in the pond at the bottom of his garden. He had rabbits in the pantry, white mice in his piano, a squirrel in the linen closet and a hedgehog in the cellar. He had a cow with a calf, too, and an old lame horse and chickens and pigeons and two lambs and many other animals. But his favorite pets were Dab-Dab the duck, Jip the dog, Gub-Gub the baby pig, Polynesia the parrot, and the owl, Too-Too.

His sister grumbled about all these animals. She said they made the house untidy. And one day an old lady came to see the Doctor and she sat on the hedgehog who was sleeping on the sofa. The old lady never came to see the Doctor after that.

Then his sister, Sarah Dolittle, came to him and said, "John, sick people will not come and see you when you keep all these animals in the house. We are getting poorer every day because the best people will not come here."

"But I like the animals better than the 'best people,' " said the Doctor.

"You are ridiculous," said his sister, and walked out of the room.

So, as time went on, the Doctor got more and more animals. And fewer and fewer people came to see him. Till at last no one came—except Matthew Mugg, the catfood man, who didn't mind any kind of animals. But the catfood man wasn't very rich and he only got sick once a year—at Christmas time. Even then he only gave the Doctor sixpence for a bottle of medicine.

Sixpence a year wasn't enough to live on—even in those days, long ago. If the Doctor hadn't had some money saved up in his money box, no one knows what would have happened.

And he kept on getting still more pets, and of course it cost a lot to feed them. And the money he had saved up grew littler and littler.

Then he sold his piano and let the mice live in a dresser drawer. But the money he got for that didn't last very long. So he sold the brown suit he wore on Sundays and went on becoming poorer and poorer.

And now, when he walked down the street in his high hat, people would say to one another, "There goes John Dolittle, M.D.! There was a time when he was the best known doctor in the West Country. Look at him now. He has no money and his stockings are full of holes!"

But the dogs and the cats and the children still ran up and followed him through the town—the same as they had done when he was rich.

# CHAPTER TWO

## Animal Language

It happened one day that the Doctor was sitting in his kitchen talking with the catfood man, who had come to see him with a stomach ache.

"Why don't you give up being a people's doctor, and be an animal doctor?" asked the catfood man.

The parrot, Polynesia, was sitting in the window. She was looking out at the rain, singing a sailor song. Then she stopped and started to listen.

"You see, Doctor," the catfood man went on, "you know all about animals—much more than what these here vets do. That book you wrote about cats—why, it's wonderful! You might have been a cat yourself. You know the way they think.

And, listen… You can make a lot of money doctoring animals. Do you know that? You see, I'd send all the old women who had sick cats or dogs to you."

"Do they get sick often?" asked the good doctor.

"All the time," answered the catfood man, "because the old women always give 'em too much to eat. And look, all the farmers 'round about who had lame horses and weak lambs—they'd come. Be an animal doctor."

When the catfood man had gone, the parrot flew off the window onto the Doctor's table and said, "That man's got sense. That's what you ought to do. Be an animal doctor. Give the silly people up. They haven't brains enough to see you're the best doctor in the world. Take care of animals instead—*they*'ll soon find it out. Be an animal doctor."

"Oh, there are plenty of animal doctors," said John Dolittle, putting the flowerpots outside on the windowsill to get the rain.

"Yes, there are plenty," said Polynesia. "But none of them are any good at all. Now, listen, Doctor, and I'll tell you something. Did you know that animals can talk?"

# THE STORY OF
# DOCTOR DOLITTLE

"I knew that parrots can talk," said the Doctor.

"Oh, we parrots can talk in two languages—people's language and bird language," said Polynesia proudly. "If I say, 'Polly wants a cracker,' you understand me. But hear this: *Ka-ka oi-ee, fee-fee?*"

"Good gracious!" cried the Doctor. "What does that mean?"

"That means, 'Is the porridge hot yet?'—in bird language."

"My! You don't say so!" said the Doctor. "You never talked that way to me before."

"You wouldn't have understood me if I had," said Polynesia.

"Tell me some more," said the Doctor, all excited. He rushed over to the dresser drawer and came back with a writing book and a pencil. "Now, don't go too fast—and I'll write it down. This is interesting—very interesting—something quite new. Give me the Birds' ABCs first—slowly, now."

So that was the way the Doctor came to know that animals had a language of their own and could talk to one another. And all that afternoon, while it was raining, Polynesia sat on the kitchen table giving him bird words to put down in the book.

# THE STORY OF
# DOCTOR DOLITTLE

At tea time, when the dog, Jip, came in, the parrot said to the Doctor, "See, *he's* talking to you."

"Looks to me as though he were scratching his ear," said the Doctor.

"But animals don't always speak with their mouths," said the parrot in a high voice, raising her eyebrows. "They talk with their ears, with their feet, with their tails—with everything. Sometimes they don't *want* to make a noise. Do you see now the way he's twitching up one side of his nose?"

"What's that mean?" asked the Doctor.

"That means, 'Can't you see that it has stopped raining?' " Polynesia answered. "He is asking you a question. Dogs nearly always use their noses for asking questions."

After a while, with the parrot's help, the Doctor got to learn the language of the animals so well that he could talk to them himself and understand everything they said. Then he decided to give up being a people's doctor.

As soon as the catfood man had told everyone that John Dolittle was going to be an animal doctor, old ladies began to bring him their pet pugs and poodles who had eaten too much cake. Farmers came many miles to show him sick cows and sheep.

# THE STORY OF
# DOCTOR DOLITTLE

One day a plow horse was brought to him. The poor thing was terribly glad to find a man who could talk in horse language.

"You know, Doctor," said the horse, "that vet over the hill knows nothing at all. He has been treating me six weeks now for bad knees. What I need is *glasses*, same as people. But that vet over the hill never even looked at my eyes. He kept on giving me big pills. I tried to tell him, but he couldn't understand a word of horse language. What I need is glasses."

"Of course, of course," said the Doctor. "I'll get you some at once."

"I would like a pair like yours," said the horse, "—only green. They'll keep the sun out of my eyes while I'm plowing the fifty-acre field."

"Certainly," said the Doctor. "Green ones you shall have. I'll have them for you next week. Come in again Tuesday. Good morning!"

Then John Dolittle got a fine, big pair of green glasses. And the plow horse stopped going blind in one eye and could see as well as ever.

And soon it became a common sight to see farm animals wearing glasses in the country around Puddleby.

And so it was with all the other animals that were brought to the Doctor. As soon as they found that he could talk their language, they told him where the pain was and how they felt, and of course it was easy for him to cure them.

Now, all these animals went back and told their brothers and friends about the good doctor with the big garden. And whenever any creatures got sick they came at once to his house, so that his big garden was nearly always crowded with animals

trying to get in to see him. Horses and cows and dogs came. And even little things of the fields came, like harvest mice and badgers and bats.

There were so many that came that he had to have special doors made for the different kinds. He wrote HORSES over the front door, COWS over the side door, and SHEEP on the kitchen door. Each kind of animal had a separate door. Even the mice had a tiny tunnel into the cellar, where they waited in rows for the Doctor to see to them.

And so, in a few years' time, every living thing for miles and miles knew about John Dolittle, M.D. And the birds who flew to other countries in the winter told the animals in far-away lands of the wonderful doctor of Puddleby-on-the-Marsh. They told how he understood their talk and could help them in their troubles. In this way he became famous among the animals all over the world. And he was happy and liked his life very much.

One afternoon, the Doctor was busy writing in a book. Polynesia sat in the window—as she nearly always did—looking out at the leaves blowing about in the garden. Then she laughed aloud.

"What is it, Polynesia?" asked the Doctor, looking up from his book.

"I was just thinking," said the parrot, and she went on looking at the leaves.

"What were you thinking?"

"I was thinking about people," said Polynesia. "People think they're so wonderful. The world has been going on now for thousands of years, hasn't it? And the only thing in animal language that *people* have learned to understand is that when a dog wags his tail he means 'I'm glad!' It's funny, isn't it? You are the very first man to talk like us!"

# THE STORY OF
# DOCTOR DOLITTLE

"You're a wise old bird," said the Doctor. "How old are you really? I know that parrots and elephants sometimes live to be very, very old."

"I can never be quite sure of my age," said Polynesia. "I lost track when I made the long trip from Africa. It's either a hundred and eighty-three or a hundred and eighty-two. Either way, I'm *still* quite young, you know…"

# CHAPTER THREE

# More Money Troubles

And soon now the Doctor began to make money again. His sister, Sarah, bought a new dress and was happy.

Some of the animals who came to see him were so sick that they had to stay at the Doctor's house for a week. And when they were getting better they used to sit in chairs on the lawn.

And often even after they got well, they did not want to go away. They liked the Doctor and his house so much. And he never had the heart to refuse them when they asked if they could stay with him. So in this way he went on getting more and more pets.

# THE STORY OF
## DOCTOR DOLITTLE

Once when the Doctor was sitting on his garden wall, an organ grinder came around with a monkey on a string. The Doctor saw at once that the monkey's collar was too tight and that he was dirty and unhappy. So he took the monkey away from the organ grinder, gave the man a coin and told him to go. The monkey stayed with Doctor Dolittle and had a good home. The other animals in the house called him "Chee-Chee"—which is a common word in monkey language, meaning "ginger."

And another time, when the circus came to Puddleby, the crocodile, who had a bad toothache, escaped at night and came into the Doctor's garden. The Doctor talked to him in crocodile language and took him into the house and made his tooth better. But when the crocodile saw what a nice house it was, he wanted to live with the Doctor, too. He asked if he could sleep in the fishpond if he promised not to eat the fish. When the circus men came to take him back, he got so wild and savage that he frightened them away. But to everyone in the house he was always as gentle as a kitten.

But now the old ladies grew afraid to send their lap dogs to Doctor Dolittle because of the crocodile. The farmers wouldn't believe that he would not eat the lambs and sick calves they brought to be cured. So the Doctor went to the crocodile and told him he must go back to his circus. But he wept such big tears, and begged so hard to stay, that the Doctor didn't have the heart to make him leave.

So then the Doctor's sister came to him and said, "John, you must send that creature away. Now the farmers and old ladies are afraid to send their animals to you. Now we shall be poor again. This is the last straw. I will no longer be housekeeper for you if you don't send away that alligator."

"It isn't an alligator," said the Doctor, "it's a crocodile."

"I don't care what you call it," said his sister. "It's an awful thing to find under the bed. I won't have it in the house."

"But he has promised me," the Doctor answered, "that he will not bite anyone. He doesn't like the circus. And I don't have the money to send him back to Africa where he comes from. He minds his own business and he is very well behaved. Don't be so fussy."

# THE STORY OF
# DOCTOR DOLITTLE

"I tell you I *will* not have him around," said Sarah. "He eats the kitchen flooring. If you don't send him away this minute I'll—I'll go and get married!"

"All right," said the Doctor, "go and get married. It can't be helped." And he put on his hat and went out into the garden.

So Sarah Dolittle packed up her things and went off, and the Doctor was left all alone with his animal family.

And very soon he was poorer than he had ever been before. With all these mouths to fill, and the house to look after, things began to look very difficult. But the Doctor didn't worry at all.

"Money is a nuisance," he used to say. "We'd all be much better off if it had never been invented. What does money matter, so long as we are happy?"

But soon the animals themselves began to get worried. And one evening they began talking it over among themselves in whispers. And the owl, Too-Too, who was good at math, figured it out that there was only money enough left to last another week—if they each had one meal a day and no more.

Then the parrot said, "I think we all should do the housework ourselves. At least we can do that much."

So it was agreed that the monkey, Chee-Chee, was to do the cooking and mending. The dog was to sweep the floors. The duck was to dust and make the beds. The owl, Too-Too, was to do the bookkeeping. And the pig was to do the gardening. They made Polynesia, the parrot, do housekeeping and laundry because she was the oldest.

Of course at first they all found their new jobs very hard to do—all except Chee-Chee, who had hands, and could do things like a man. But they soon got used to it. They thought it was great fun to watch Jip, the dog, sweeping his tail over the floor with a rag tied onto it for a broom. After a little while, they did the work so well that the Doctor said he had never had his house kept so tidy or so clean before.

In this way things went along all right for a while. But without money they found it very hard.

Then the animals made a vegetable and flower stand outside the garden gate and sold radishes and roses to the people that passed by along the road.

# THE STORY OF
# DOCTOR DOLITTLE

But still they didn't seem to make enough money to pay all the bills. And still the Doctor wouldn't worry. When the parrot came to him and told him that the fish seller wouldn't give them any more fish, he said, "Never mind. So long as the hens lay eggs and the cow gives milk we can have omelets and creamy cheese. And there are plenty of vegetables left in the garden. The Winter is still a long way off. Don't fuss!"

But the snow came early that year. The old lame horse hauled in wood from the forest outside the town so they could have a big fire in the kitchen. Still, most of the vegetables in the garden were gone, and the rest were covered with snow. And many of the animals were really hungry.

# CHAPTER FOUR

# A Message from Africa

One cold Winter night, they were all sitting around the warm fire in the kitchen. The Doctor was reading aloud to them out of books he had written in animal language. Suddenly, the owl, Too-Too, said, "Sh! What's that noise outside?"

They all listened and heard the sound of someone running. Then the door flew open and the monkey, Chee-Chee, ran in, badly out of breath.

"Doctor!" he cried. "I have a message from my cousin in Africa. There is a bad sickness among the monkeys there. They are all catching it—and they are dying in hundreds. They have heard of you, and beg you to come to Africa to stop the sickness."

"Who brought the message?" asked the Doctor. He took off his glasses and put down his book.

"A swallow," said Chee-Chee. "She is outside."

"Bring her in by the fire," said the Doctor. "She must be very cold. The swallows flew South six weeks ago!"

So the swallow was brought in. She was a little afraid at first and shivering. But she soon warmed up and sat on the mantel and began to talk.

When she had finished, the Doctor said, "I would gladly go to Africa. But I'm afraid we don't have money enough to buy the tickets to get there. Get me the money box, Chee-Chee."

The monkey climbed up and got it off the dresser. There was nothing in it—not one penny!

"I felt *sure* there was a twopence left," said the Doctor.

"There *was*," said the owl, "but you spent it on a rattle for that otter's baby when he was teething."

"Did I?" said the Doctor. "Dear me, dear me! What a nuisance money is, to be sure! Well, never mind. I will go down to the seaside to try to borrow a boat that will take us to Africa. I knew a sailor once who brought his baby to me with measles. Maybe he'll lend us his boat, since the baby got well."

So early the next morning the Doctor went down to the seashore. And when he came back he told the animals it was all right. The sailor was going to lend them the boat.

Then the crocodile and the monkey and the parrot were very glad and began to sing. For they were going back to Africa, their real home. And the Doctor said, "I shall only be able to take you three— with Jip the dog, Dab-Dab the duck, Gub-Gub the pig, and the owl, Too-Too. The rest of the animals, like the mice and the bats, they will have to go back and live in the fields till we come home again. But as most of them sleep through the Winter, they won't mind that."

The parrot had been on long sea voyages before. So she began telling the Doctor all the things he would have to take with him on the ship.

"You must have plenty of thick crackers," she said. "And you must have food in cans. And an anchor."

"I think the ship will have its own anchor," said the Doctor.

"Well, make sure," said Polynesia. "Because it's very important. You can't stop if you haven't got an anchor. And you'll need a bell."

"What's that for?" asked the Doctor.

"To tell the time by," said the parrot. "You go and ring it every half-hour and then you know what time it is. And bring a whole lot of rope. It always comes in handy on voyages."

Then they began to wonder where they were going to get the money from to buy all the things they needed.

"Oh, bother it! Money again," cried the Doctor. "Goodness! I shall be glad to get to the jungles of Africa where we don't have to have any! I'll go and ask the food store man if he will wait for his money till I get back. No, I'll send the sailor to ask him."

So the sailor went to the food store. And soon he came back with all the things they wanted.

Then the animals packed up. They turned off the water so the pipes wouldn't freeze. They closed the shutters. They locked the house and gave the key to the old horse in the stable. They made sure there was plenty of hay in the loft to last the horse through Winter. Then they carried all their bags down to the seashore and got onto the boat.

The catfood man was there to see them off. He brought a large basket of biscuits as a present for the Doctor and the animals.

As soon as they were on the ship, Gub-Gub the baby pig asked where the beds were. It was four o'clock in the afternoon and he wanted his nap. So Polynesia took him downstairs into the inside of the ship and showed him the beds. They were all on top of one another like bookshelves on a wall.

"Why, that isn't a bed!" cried Gub-Gub. "That's a shelf!"

"Beds are always like that on ships," said the parrot. "It isn't a shelf. Climb up into it and go to sleep. That's what you call 'a bunk.'"

"I don't think I'll go to bed yet," said Gub-Gub. "I'm too excited. I want to go upstairs again and see them start."

"Well, this is your first trip," said Polynesia. "You will get used to the life after a while." And she went back up the stairs of the ship, humming a sailor song.

They were just going to start on their journey, when the Doctor said he would have to go back and ask the sailor the way to Africa.

But the swallow said she had been to that country many times and would show them how to get there.

So the Doctor told Chee-Chee to pull up the anchor—and the voyage began.

# CHAPTER FIVE

# The Great Journey

Now, for six whole weeks they went sailing on and on, over the rolling sea. They followed the swallow, who flew before the ship to show them the way. At night she carried a tiny lantern, so they would not miss her in the dark. And the people on the other ships that passed said that the light must be a shooting star.

As they sailed further and further into the South, it got warmer and warmer. Polynesia, Chee-Chee, and the crocodile enjoyed the hot sun. They ran about laughing and looking over the side of the ship to see if they could see Africa yet. But the pig and the dog and the owl, Too-Too, were too hot.

They sat at the end of the ship in the shade of a big barrel, with their tongues hanging out, drinking lemonade. Dab-Dab kept herself cool by jumping into the sea and swimming behind the ship.

When they got near to the Equator they saw some flying-fish coming toward them. And the fishes asked the parrot if this was Doctor Dolittle's ship. She told them it was. They said they were glad, because the monkeys in Africa were getting worried that he would never come. Polynesia asked them how many miles they had yet to go. And the flying-fish said it was only fifty-five miles now to the coast of Africa.

And another time a school of porpoises came dancing through the waves. They also asked Polynesia if this was the ship of the famous doctor. Then they asked the parrot if the Doctor wanted anything for his journey.

Polynesia said, "Yes. We are short of onions."

"There is an island not far from here," said the porpoises, "where the wild onions grow tall and strong. We will get some and catch up to you."

So the porpoises dashed away through the sea. Very soon they came up behind, dragging onions through the waves in big nets made of seaweed.

The next evening, as the sun was going down, the Doctor said, "Get me the telescope, Chee-Chee. Our journey is nearly ended. Very soon we should be able to see the shores of Africa."

And, sure enough, about half an hour later, they thought they could see land. But it began to get darker and darker and they couldn't be sure. Then a great storm came up, with thunder and lightning. The wind howled and the rain came down hard. The waves got so high they splashed right over the boat.

Soon there was a big *bang*! The ship stopped and rolled over on its side.

The Doctor ran up from downstairs. "What's happened?" he asked.

"I'm not sure," said the parrot, "but I think we're shipwrecked. Tell the duck to get out and see."

So Dab-Dab dove right down under the waves. And when she came up she said they had struck a rock. There was a big hole in the bottom of the ship. The water was coming in, and they were sinking fast.

"We must have run into Africa," said the Doctor. "Dear me! Well, we must all swim to land."

# THE STORY OF
# DOCTOR DOLITTLE

But Chee-Chee and Gub-Gub did not know how to swim.

"Get the rope!" said Polynesia. "I told you it would come in handy. Where's that duck? Come here, Dab-Dab. Take this end of the rope, fly to the shore and tie it onto a palm tree. We'll hold the other end on the ship here. Anyone who can't swim must climb along the rope till they reach the land. That's what you call a 'life line.'"

So they all got safely to the shore. Chee-Chee and Gub-Gub brought the Doctor's trunk and handbag with them.

But the ship was no good anymore with the big hole in the bottom. Soon the rough sea beat it to pieces on the rocks and those pieces floated away.

They all took shelter till the storm was over in a nice dry cave they found high up in the cliffs.

When the sun came out the next morning they went down to the sandy beach to dry themselves.

"Dear old Africa!" sighed Polynesia. "It's good to get back. Just think—it'll be a hundred and sixty-nine years tomorrow since I was here! And it hasn't changed a bit! Same old palm trees. Same old red earth. Same old black ants! There's no place like home!"

And the others noticed she had tears in her eyes. She was so pleased to see her country once again.

Then the Doctor realized his high hat was missing. It had been blown into the sea during the storm. So Dab-Dab went out to look for it. And soon she saw it, a long way off, floating on the water like a toy boat. When she flew down to get it, she found one of the white mice sitting inside it. It was very frightened.

"What are you doing here?" asked the duck. "You were told to stay behind in Puddleby."

"I didn't want to be left behind," said the mouse. "I wanted to see what Africa was like. I have relatives there. So I hid and was brought onto the ship with the crackers. When the ship sank I was terribly frightened because I cannot swim far. I swam as long as I could, but I got very tired and thought I was going to sink. Then the old man's hat came floating by and I got into it because I did not want to be drowned."

So the duck brought the hat with the mouse in it to the Doctor on the shore. And they all gathered round to have a look.

"That's what you call a 'stow-away,' " said the parrot.

Suddenly the monkey, Chee-Chee, said, "Sh! I hear footsteps in the jungle!"

They all stopped talking and listened. And soon an African man came down out of the woods and asked them what they were doing there.

"My name is John Dolittle—M. D.," said the Doctor. "I have been asked to come to Africa to cure the monkeys who are sick."

"You must all come before the King," said the man.

"What king?" asked the Doctor.

"The King of the Jolliginki," the man answered. "All these lands belong to him. All strangers must be brought before him. Follow me."

So they gathered up their baggage and went off, following the man through the jungle.

# CHAPTER SIX

# Polynesia and the King

They all went a little way through the thick forest. Then they came to a wide, clear space. There they saw the King's palace made of mud.

This was where the King lived with his Queen, Ermintrude, and their son, Prince Bumpo. The Prince was away fishing for salmon in the river. But the King and Queen were sitting under an umbrella before the palace door. The Queen was asleep.

The Doctor came up to the palace and told the King why he had come to Africa.

"You may not travel through my lands," said the King. "Many years ago an Englishman came to these shores, and I was very kind to him.

But he dug holes in the ground to get gold. And he killed all the elephants to get their ivory tusks. Then he went away secretly in his ship without even saying 'Thank you.' Never again shall an Englishman travel through the lands of Jolliginki."

Then the King turned to some of his soldiers. "Take away this medicine-man—with all his animals," he said, "and lock them up in my strongest prison."

So six of the soldiers led the Doctor and all his pets away and shut them up in a stone dungeon. The dungeon had only one little window. It was high up in the wall, with bars in it. And the door was strong and thick.

They all grew very sad, and Gub-Gub the pig began to cry.

"Are we all here?" asked the Doctor.

"Yes, I think so," said the duck.

"Where's Polynesia?" asked the crocodile. "She isn't here."

"Are you sure?" said the Doctor. "Look again. Polynesia! Polynesia! Where are you?"

"I suppose she escaped. Well, that's just like her!" grumbled the crocodile. "She sneaked off into the jungle as soon as her friends got into trouble."

# THE STORY OF
# DOCTOR DOLITTLE

"I'm not that kind of a bird," said a voice. Then the parrot climbed out of the pocket in the tail of the Doctor's coat. "You see, I was afraid they would put me in a small cage. So while the King was busy talking, I hid in the Doctor's pocket—and here I am! That's what you call a 'ruse,' " she said. She smoothed down her feathers with her beak.

"Good gracious!" cried the Doctor. "You're lucky I didn't sit on you."

"Now, listen," said Polynesia. "Tonight, as soon as it gets dark, I am going to creep through the bars of that window and fly over to the palace. And then—you'll see—I'll soon find a way to make the King let us all out of prison."

"Oh, what can *you* do?" said Gub-Gub. He turned up his nose and began to cry again. "You're only a bird!"

"Quite true," said the parrot. "But do not forget that although I am only a bird, *I can talk like a man.* And I know these people."

That night, when the moon was shining through the palm trees and all the King's men were asleep, the parrot slipped out and flew to the palace. She popped in through a hole in the pantry window. (It had been broken by a tennis ball the week before.)

Then she tiptoed up the stairs till she came to the King's bedroom. She opened the door gently and peeped in. The Queen was away at a dance that night at her cousin's. But the King was in bed fast asleep. Polynesia crept in, very softly, and got under the bed. Then she coughed—just the way Doctor Dolittle would cough. She could sound like anyone.

The King opened his eyes and said sleepily, "Is that you, Ermintrude?"

Then the parrot coughed again—loud, like a man. And the King sat up, wide awake, and said, "Who's that?"

"I am Doctor Dolittle," said the parrot.

"What are you doing in my bedroom?" cried the King. "How dare you get out of prison! Where are you? I don't see you."

But the parrot just laughed—a long, deep, jolly laugh, like the Doctor's.

"Stop laughing and come here at once, so I can see you," said the King.

"Foolish King!" answered Polynesia. "Have you forgotten that you are talking to John Dolittle, M.D.—the most wonderful man on earth? Of course you cannot see me. I have made myself invisible. There is nothing I cannot do. Now, listen. I have come here tonight to warn you. If you don't let me and my animals travel through your kingdom, I will make you and all your people sick. For I can make people well, and I can make people ill—just by raising my little finger. Send your soldiers at once to open the dungeon door, or you shall have mumps before the morning sun has risen on the hills of Jolliginki."

Then the King began to tremble and was very much afraid.

"As you wish, Doctor," he cried. "Do not raise your little finger, please!" He jumped out of bed and ran to tell the soldiers to open the prison door.

As soon as the King was gone, Polynesia crept downstairs and left by the pantry window.

But the Queen, who was just letting herself in at the back door with a key, saw the parrot getting out through the broken glass. And when the King came back to bed she told him what she had seen.

Then the King understood that he had been tricked, and he was very angry. He hurried back to the prison at once—

—but he was too late. The door stood open. The dungeon was empty. The Doctor and all his animals were gone.

# CHAPTER SEVEN

# The Bridge of Apes

The Queen had never in her life seen the King so terrible as he got that night. He gnashed his teeth with rage. He threw his toothbrush at the palace cat. He rushed around in his nightshirt and woke up all his army and sent them into the jungle to catch the Doctor. Then he made all his servants go, too—his cooks and his gardeners and his barber and Prince Bumpo's tutor. He even made the Queen, who was tired from dancing in a pair of tight shoes, go help the soldiers in their search.

All this time, the Doctor and his animals were running through the forest toward the Land of the Monkeys as fast as they could go.

Gub-Gub soon got tired and the Doctor had to carry him. This made it pretty hard when they had the trunk and the handbag with them as well.

The King of the Jolliginki thought his army could find them easily, because the Doctor was in a strange land and would not know his way. But he was wrong. For Chee-Chee knew all the paths through the jungle. He led the Doctor and his pets to the very thickest part of the forest and hid them all in a big hollow tree between high rocks.

"We had better wait here," said Chee-Chee, "till the soldiers have gone back to bed. Then we can go on into the Land of the Monkeys."

So there they stayed the whole night through. They often heard the King's men searching and talking in the jungle. But they were quite safe, for no one knew of that hiding place but Chee-Chee— not even the other monkeys.

At last daylight began to come through the thick leaves overhead. Chee-Chee brought the Doctor and his animals out of the hiding place and they set off for the Land of the Monkeys.

It was a long, long way, and they often got very tired. They always had plenty to eat and drink because Chee-Chee and Polynesia knew all the different kinds of fruits and vegetables that grow in the jungle. They knew where to find the dates and figs and groundnuts and ginger and yams. They knew how to make lemonade out of the juice of wild oranges, sweetened with honey from the bees' nests in hollow trees.

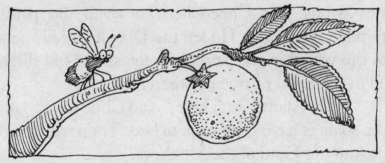

At night they slept in tents made of palm leaves, on thick, soft beds of dried grass. And after a while they got used to walking such a lot and did not get so tired and enjoyed the life of travel very much.

But they were always glad when the night came and they stopped for their resting time. Then the Doctor would make a little fire of sticks. And after they had their supper, they would sit around it in a ring. Polynesia sang songs about the sea. Chee-Chee told stories of the jungle.

One day Chee-Chee climbed up a high rock and looked out over the treetops. And when he came down he said they were now quite close to the Land of the Monkeys and would soon be there.

And that same evening, sure enough, they saw Chee-Chee's cousin! They saw a lot of other monkeys sitting in the trees by the edge of a swamp. They had been looking and waiting for them. And when they saw the famous Doctor really coming, these monkeys cheered and waved leaves and swung out of the branches to greet him.

They wanted to carry his bag and his trunk and everything he had. One of the bigger monkeys even carried Gub-Gub. Then two of them rushed on in front to tell the sick monkeys that the Great Doctor had come at last.

But the King's men, who were still following, had heard the noise of the monkeys cheering. They at last knew where the Doctor was, and ran on to catch him.

The big monkey carrying Gub-Gub was coming along behind slowly, and he saw the Captain of the army sneaking through the trees. So he hurried after the Doctor and told him to run.

Then they all ran harder than they had ever run in their lives. And the King's men began to run, too. The Captain ran hardest of all.

Chee-Chee shouted, "We haven't far to go now!"

But before they could get into the Land of the Monkeys, they came to a steep cliff with a river flowing below. This was the end of the Kingdom of Jolliginki. The Land of the Monkeys was on the other side—across the river.

And Jip the dog looked down over the edge of the steep, steep cliff and said, "Golly! How are we ever going to get across?"

"Oh, dear!" said Gub-Gub. "The King's men are quite close now. Look at them! I am afraid we are going to be taken back to prison again." And he began to weep.

But the big monkey who was carrying the pig dropped him on the ground and cried out to the other monkeys.

"Boys—a bridge! Quick! Make a bridge! We've only a minute to do it. A bridge! A bridge!"

The Doctor began to wonder what they were going to make a bridge out of. He gazed around to see if they had any boards hidden any place.

But when he looked back at the cliff, there, hanging across the river, was a bridge all ready for him—made of living monkeys! For while his back

was turned, the monkeys—quick as a flash—had made themselves into a bridge, just by holding hands and feet.

And the big one shouted to the Doctor, "Walk over! Walk over—all of you—hurry!"

Gub-Gub was a bit scared to walk on such a narrow bridge at a dizzy height above the river! But he got over all right, and so did all of them.

John Dolittle was the last to cross. And just as he was getting to the other side, the King's men came rushing up to the edge of the cliff.

Then they shook their fists and yelled with rage. For they saw they were too late. The Doctor and all his animals were safe in the Land of the Monkeys and the bridge was pulled across to the other side.

Then Chee-Chee turned to the Doctor and said, "Many great explorers have hidden in the jungle for weeks hoping to see the monkeys do that trick. But we never let an Englishman see it before. You are the first to see the famous 'Bridge of Apes.'"

And the Doctor felt very pleased.

# CHAPTER EIGHT

# A Lion's Pride and Monkeys' Council

John Dolittle now became quite busy. He found hundreds and thousands of sick monkeys. There were gorillas, orangutans, chimpanzees, baboons, gray monkeys, red ones—all kinds. Many had died.

He separated the sick ones from the well ones. Then he got Chee-Chee and his cousin to build him a little house of grass. Next he made all the monkeys who were still well come and be vaccinated. And for three days and three nights the monkeys kept coming from the jungles and the valleys and the hills to the little house of grass. The Doctor sat all day and all night, vaccinating and vaccinating.

Then he had another big house made with a lot of beds in it. He put all the sick ones in this house.

But so many were sick, there were not enough well ones to do the nursing. So he sent messages to the other animals, like the lions and the leopards and the antelopes, to come and help.

But the Leader of the Lions was a very proud creature. And when he came to the Doctor's big house full of beds he was angry and prideful.

"Do you dare to ask me, sir?" he said, glaring at the Doctor. "Do you dare to ask me—*me, the King of the Beasts*, to wait on a lot of dirty monkeys?"

Although the lion looked very terrible, the Doctor tried hard not to seem afraid of him.

"They're not dirty," he said quietly. "They've all had a bath this morning. *Your* coat looks as though it could use a brushing. Now, listen, and I'll tell you something. The day may come when the lions get sick. If you don't help the other animals *now*, the lions may find themselves all alone when *they* are in trouble. That often happens to proud people."

"The lions are never *in* trouble—they only *make* trouble," said the Leader, turning up his nose. And he stalked away into the jungle. He felt he had been rather smart and clever.

But when he got back to his den, the Leader of the Lions saw his wife, the Queen Lioness, come running out to meet him.

"One of the cubs won't eat," she said. "I don't know *what* to do with him. He hasn't taken a thing since last night."

So the Leader went into his den and looked at his two little cubs, lying on the floor. And one of them seemed quite ill.

Then the lion told his wife, quite proudly, what he had just said to the Doctor. And she got so angry she nearly drove him out of the den.

"How could you?" she screamed. "All the animals from here to the Indian Ocean are talking about this wonderful man. They say he can cure any kind of sickness. They say he is very kind. He is the only man in the whole world who can talk the language of the animals! And now you have refused to help him? We have a sick baby on our hands! Go back to that man at once," she yelled, "and tell him you're sorry. And take all the other lions with you. Then do everything the Doctor tells you. Work hard! And perhaps he will be kind enough to come and see the cub later. Now be off! *Hurry*, I tell you! You're not fit to be a father!"

So the Leader of the Lions went back to the Doctor and said he was very sorry. Then the Doctor was happy, for all the lions and the leopards and the antelopes and the giraffes and the zebras came to help him in his work. The Doctor went to see the cub and gave him some medicine, so all was well.

And now very soon the monkeys began to get better. At the end of a week the big house full of beds was half empty. And at the end of the second week the last monkey had gotten well.

Then the Doctor's work was done. He was so tired he went to bed and slept for three days without even turning over.

Chee-Chee stood outside the Doctor's door, keeping everybody away till he woke up.

Then John Dolittle told the monkeys that he must now go back to Puddleby.

They were very surprised at this, for they had thought that he was going to stay with them forever. And that night all the monkeys got together in the jungle to talk it over.

The Chief Chimpanzee rose up and said, "Why is the good man going away? Is he not happy here with us?"

But none of them could answer him.

Then the Grand Gorilla got up and said, "I think we all should go to him and ask him to stay. Perhaps if we make him a new house and a bigger bed he will not wish to go."

Then Chee-Chee got up. All the others whispered, "Sh! Look! Chee-Chee, the Great Traveler, is about to speak!"

"My friends," said Chee-Chee, "I am afraid it is useless to ask the Doctor to stay. He owes money in Puddleby and he says he must go back and pay it."

And the monkeys asked him, "What is *money*?"

Then Chee-Chee told them that in the Land of England you could get nothing without money. You could *do* nothing without money. It was almost impossible to *live* without money.

"When we were coming to you we had to bring food," Chee-Chee said, "but we had no money. We said we would pay when we came back. And we borrowed a boat from a sailor. But it was broken on the rocks when we reached Africa. Now the Doctor says he must go back and get the sailor another boat. The man was poor. His ship was all he had."

And the monkeys were all silent for a while, sitting quite still upon the ground and thinking quite hard.

At last the Biggest Baboon got up and said, "I do not think we ought to let this good man leave our land till we have given him a fine present to take with him. For we are grateful for all that he has done for us."

And then they all cried out, making a great noise, "Yes, yes. Let us give him the finest present!"

"Fifty bags of coconuts!" said one.

"A hundred bunches of bananas!" said another.

But Chee-Chee told them that all these things

would be too heavy to carry so far and would go bad before half was eaten.

"If you want to please him," he said, "give him an animal. He will be kind to it. Give him some rare animal they don't have in the zoos."

And the monkeys asked him, "What are *zoos*?"

Then Chee-Chee explained to them that zoos were places in the Land of England where animals were put in cages for people to come and look at. And the monkeys were very shocked.

"Have they an iguana over there?" one said.

Chee-Chee said, "Yes, there is an iguana in the London Zoo."

And another asked, "Have they got an okapi?"

"Yes," said Chee-Chee.

And another stood up and asked, "Have they got a pushmi-pullyu?"

"No. No one from the Land of England has ever seen a pushmi-pullyu," said Chee-Chee. "Let us give him that."

# CHAPTER NINE

# The Rarest Animal of All

Pushmi-pullyus are now extinct. That means there aren't any more. But long ago, when Doctor Dolittle was alive, there were some of them still left in the deepest jungles of Africa. They had no tail. They had two heads—one at each end. Each head had sharp horns. They were very shy and hard to catch. You could not sneak up behind one to catch him while he wasn't looking. No matter which way you came toward him, he was always facing you. And besides, only one half of him slept at a time. The other head was always awake—and watching. This was why they were never caught and never seen in zoos.

Well, the monkeys set out to find this animal. And after they had gone many miles, one of them found strange footprints near the edge of a river. They knew that a pushmi-pullyu must be very near that spot.

Then they went along the riverbank a little way. They saw a place where the grass was high and thick, and they guessed that he was in there.

So they all joined hands and made a great circle around the high grass. The pushmi-pullyu heard them coming. He tried hard to break through the ring of monkeys, but he couldn't do it. When he saw that it was no use trying to escape, he sat down and waited to see what they wanted.

They asked him if he would go with Doctor Dolittle and be in a show in the Land of England.

He shook both his heads at once and said, "Certainly not!"

They explained to him that he would not be shut up in a zoo, but would just be looked at. They told him that the Doctor was a very kind man but he had no money. They said that people would pay to see a two-headed animal. The Doctor would get rich and could pay for the boat he had borrowed to come to Africa in.

# THE STORY OF
# DOCTOR DOLITTLE

But he answered, "No. You know how shy I am. I hate being stared at." And he almost began to cry.

Then for three days they tried to get him to go with the Doctor. And at the end of the third day he said he would come with them and first see what kind of a man the Doctor was.

So the monkeys traveled back with the pushmi-pullyu. And when they came to the Doctor's little house of grass, they took him in.

"What in the world is it?" asked John Dolittle.

"My, my!" cried the duck. "How does it make up its mind?"

"This, Doctor," said Chee-Chee, "is the pushmi-pullyu, the rarest animal of the African jungles. The only two-headed beast in the world! Take him home with you and you will be rich. People will pay any money to see him."

"But I don't want any money," said the Doctor.

"Yes, you do," said Dab-Dab the duck. "Don't you remember how poor we were before? And how are you going to get the sailor a new boat?"

"I was going to make him one," said the Doctor.

"Oh, really, now!" cried Dab-Dab. "Where would you get all the wood and nails? Take the funny-looking thing and make some money with a show!"

"Well, perhaps…" said the Doctor. "It certainly would make a nice new kind of pet. But does the—er—what-do-you-call-it really want to go to England?"

The pushmi-pullyu saw at once that he could trust the Doctor. "Yes, I'll go," he said. "You have been so kind to the animals here. And the monkeys tell me that I am the only one who will do. But you must promise me that if I do not like it in England you will send me back."

"Why, of course, of course," said the Doctor. "Excuse me, surely you are from the Deer Family, are you not?"

"Yes," said the pushmi-pullyu, "from the Ethiopian Gazelles and the Asian Goats on my mother's side. My father's great-grandfather was the last of the Unicorns."

"Most interesting!" said the Doctor.

"I notice," said the duck, "that you only talk with one of your mouths. Can't the other head talk?"

"Oh, yes," said the pushmi-pullyu. "But I keep the other mouth for eating—mostly. In that way I can talk while I am eating without being rude. Our people have always been very polite."

The monkeys gave a grand party for the Doctor after he had packed. All the animals of the jungle came. They had pineapples and mangoes and honey and all sorts of good things to eat and drink.

After they had all finished eating, the Doctor got up and said, "My friends, I am not clever at speaking long words after dinner. And I have just eaten many fruits and much honey. I wish to tell you that I am very sad at leaving your beautiful country. But I must go, for I have things to do back in my home country. After I have gone, remember never to let the flies settle on your food before you eat it. And do not sleep on the ground when the rains are coming. I—er—er—I hope you will all live happily ever after." Then he sat down.

All the monkeys clapped their hands a long time. They said to one another, "Let it be remembered always among our people that he sat and ate with us, here, under the trees. For surely he is the Greatest of Men!"

And the Grand Gorilla, who had the strength of seven horses in his hairy arms, rolled a great rock up to the head of the table and said, "This stone for all time shall mark the spot."

And even to this day, in the heart of the Jungle, that stone still is there. And monkey mothers, passing through the forest with their families, still point down at it from the branches and whisper to their children, "Sh! There it is—look—where the Good Doctor sat and ate food with us in the Year of the Great Sickness!"

Then, when the party was over, the Doctor and his pets started out to go back to the seashore. And all the monkeys went with him as far as the edge of their country, carrying his trunk and bags, to see him off.

# CHAPTER TEN

# The Noble Deed

By the edge of the river they stopped and said farewell. This took a long time, because all those thousands of monkeys wanted to shake John Dolittle by the hand.

When they were going on alone, Polynesia said, "We must walk softly and talk low as we go through the Land of the Jolliginki. If the King hears us, he will send his soldiers to catch us again. I am sure he is still very angry over the trick I played on him."

"What I am wondering," said the Doctor, "is where we are going to get another boat to go home in… Oh, well, perhaps we'll find one lying about on the beach that nobody is using."

One day, while they were passing through a very thick part of the forest, Chee-Chee went ahead of them to look for coconuts. And while he was away, the Doctor and the animals got lost in the deep woods. They wandered around and around but could not find their way down to the seashore.

Chee-Chee, when he could not see them anywhere, was terribly upset. He climbed high trees and looked out from the top branches to try and see the Doctor's high hat. He waved and shouted. He called to all the animals by name. But it was no use. They seemed to have disappeared.

Indeed they had lost their way very badly. They had strayed a long way off the path. The jungle was so thick with bushes and vines that sometimes they could hardly move at all. The Doctor had to take out his pocketknife and cut his way along. They stumbled into wet, boggy places. They were scratched by thorns. And twice they nearly lost the medicine bag in the tangled brush. And nowhere could they come upon a path.

They blundered about like this for many days, getting their clothes torn and their faces covered with mud. Then they walked right into the King's back garden by mistake.

The King's men came running up at once and caught them. But Polynesia flew into a tree in the garden and hid herself. The Doctor and the rest were taken before the King.

"Ha, ha!" cried the King. "So you are caught again! This time you shall not escape. Take them all back to prison and put double locks on the door."

So the Doctor and his pets were led back to prison and locked up. They were all very unhappy.

"This is a great nuisance," said the Doctor. "I really must get back to Puddleby. That poor sailor will think I've stolen his ship if I don't get home soon… I wonder if those hinges are loose."

But the door was very strong and firmly locked. There seemed no chance of getting out. Then Gub-Gub began to cry again.

All this time, Polynesia was still sitting in the tree in the palace garden. Soon she spied Chee-Chee swinging through the trees, still looking for the Doctor. When Chee-Chee saw her, he came into her tree and asked her what had become of him.

"The Doctor and all the animals have been caught by the King's men and locked up again," whispered Polynesia. "We lost our way in the jungle and blundered into the palace garden by mistake."

"But couldn't you guide them?" asked Chee-Chee. He began to scold the parrot for letting them get lost while he was away looking for the coconuts.

"Sh!—Look!" said the parrot. "There's Prince Bumpo coming into the garden! He must not see us. Don't move, whatever you do!"

And there, sure enough, was young Prince Bumpo, the King's son. He was just opening the garden gate. He carried a book of fairy tales under his arm. He came strolling down the gravel walk, humming a sad song. Then he reached a stone seat right under the tree where the parrot and the monkey were hiding. He lay down on the seat and began reading the stories to himself.

Chee-Chee and Polynesia watched him, keeping very quiet and still.

After a while the King's son laid the book down and sighed a weary sigh.

"If I could only have adventures, or fight dragons, or rescue people! I want to be like the heroes I read about in my books!" he said. He had a dreamy look in his eyes.

Then the parrot began to talk in a high voice, like a girl. "Bumpo, there is a great wizard nearby who needs a hero to rescue him!"

# THE STORY OF
# DOCTOR DOLITTLE

The King's son sat up and looked all around.

"What is this I hear?" he cried. "I think it is the sweet music of a fairy's voice from the garden!"

"Brave Prince," said Polynesia, keeping very still so Bumpo couldn't see her, "your words are true. For it is I, Tripsitinka, the Queen of the Fairies. I am hiding in a rosebud."

"Oh, tell me, Fairy Queen," cried Bumpo, clasping his hands in joy, "who is it I must rescue?"

"In thy father's prison," said the parrot, "there lies a famous wizard. He is the great adventurer, Doctor John Dolittle. He knows many things about medicine and animals. He has done mighty deeds. Yet thy kingly father has locked him up by mistake. He is in need of a ship to carry him back to his homeland. Go to him, brave Bumpo. When the sun has set, go in secret and release him from prison! Prepare a ship for him and his animal crew. Do this noble deed. And someday he will take you on a grand, magical adventure! I have said enough. I must now go back to Fairyland. Farewell!"

"Farewell!" cried the Prince. "A thousand thanks, good Tripsitinka!"

And he sat down on the seat again with a smile upon his face. He was going to be a hero!

Very, very quietly Polynesia then slipped out at the back of the tree and flew across to the prison.

She found Gub-Gub poking his nose through the bars of the window. He was trying to sniff the cooking-smells that came from the palace kitchen. She told the pig to bring the Doctor to the window because she wanted to speak to him. So Gub-Gub went and woke the Doctor, who was taking a nap.

"Listen," whispered the parrot to Doctor Dolittle, "Prince Bumpo is coming here tonight to see you. He will open the prison door and find a ship for you. But you must promise to take him with you on a voyage someday."

"Well, I don't know... I suppose..." said the Doctor.

That night Prince Bumpo came secretly to the Doctor in prison and said to him, "Great Wizard, I am an unhappy prince. I have traveled the world, but I have never had an adventure like those in my storybooks. I have never fought pirates or rescued anyone! So I spend my days reading and dreaming. Now, I hear that you are a Great Adventurer. If you will take me with you I will give you half my kingdom and anything else you ask for."

"Prince Bumpo," said the Doctor kindly, "if you left your mother and father now, they would miss you terribly. And I don't want half your kingdom. I only want a ship."

"I have already prepared our ship!" whispered Prince Bumpo. "It awaits on the beach, stocked with food. It will take us all across the sea."

"My dear young man," said the Doctor slowly, "you have done brave and noble work. But I cannot take you with me. Come to England when you are older. Then we will see about an adventure. Promise you will look me up in England. Promise— by the crown of Jolliginki!"

So the Prince bowed to the Great Doctor and promised. Then Bumpo took a bunch of copper keys from his pocket and undid the great double locks. The Doctor with all his animals ran as fast as they could down to the seashore.

And Bumpo leaned against the wall of the empty dungeon, smiling a happy, noble smile.

# CHAPTER ELEVEN

# The Swallows Save the Day

When the Doctor and the animals came to the beach they saw Polynesia and Chee-Chee waiting for them on the rocks near the ship.

"I hope I did not disappoint Bumpo," said the Doctor. "He has a good heart. He promised he would look me up. I'm certain to see him again someday."

Then the pushmi-pullyu, the white mouse, Gub-Gub, Dab-Dab, Jip, and the owl, Too-Too, went onto the ship with the Doctor. But Chee-Chee, Polynesia, and the crocodile stayed behind, because Africa was their real home. It was the land where they were born.

And when the Doctor stood upon the boat, he looked over the side across the water. He remembered that they had no one to guide them back to Puddleby. The wide, wide sea looked terribly big and lonesome in the moonlight. He began to wonder if they would lose their way.

But then they heard a strange whispering noise, high in the air, coming through the night. The animals all stopped saying good-bye and listened.

The noise grew louder and bigger. It sounded like the wind blowing through the leaves of a tree, or a great, great rain beating down upon a roof.

And Jip, with his nose pointing in the air and his tail quite straight, said, "Birds!—millions of them— flying fast—that's it!"

They all looked up. And there they could see thousands and thousands of little birds. Soon the whole sky seemed full of them.

And soon all these birds flew down. They began to settle on the sands and along the ropes of the ship. The Doctor could see that they had blue wings and white bellies and very short legs. As soon as they had all found a place to sit, there was no noise left anywhere. All was quiet. All was still.

And in the silent moonlight John Dolittle spoke.
"I had no idea that we had been in Africa so long.
It will be nearly Summer when we get home. For
these are the swallows going back. Swallows, I thank
you for waiting for us. It is very thoughtful of you.
Now we will not lose our way upon the sea. Pull up
the anchor and set the sail!"

The ship moved out upon the water. Chee-Chee, Polynesia, and the crocodile felt very sad. For never in their lives had they known anyone they liked as much as Doctor John Dolittle of Puddleby-on-the-Marsh.

They called good-bye to him again and again and again. Then they stood there upon the rocks, crying and waving till the ship was out of sight.

Along the way, the Doctor's ship had to pass the coast of Barbary. It is a wild, lonely place—all sand and stones. And it was here that the Barbary pirates lived.

These pirates were a bad lot. They used to wait for sailors to be shipwrecked on their shores. And often, if they saw a boat passing, they would come out in their fast sailing ships and chase it. When they caught a boat, they would steal everything on it. After they had taken the people off they would sink the ship. Then they would sail back to Barbary singing songs and feeling proud of the mischief they had done. They made the people they had caught write home to their friends for money.

Now, one sunshiny day the Doctor and Dab-Dab were walking up and down on the ship for exercise. A nice fresh wind was blowing the boat along, and everybody was happy. Soon Dab-Dab saw the sail of another ship a long way behind them. It was a red sail.

"I don't like the look of that sail," said Dab-Dab. "I have a feeling it isn't a friendly ship."

Jip was taking a nap in the sun and he began to growl and talk in his sleep.

"I smell roast beef cooking," he mumbled. "Underdone roast beef—with brown gravy over it."

"Good gracious!" cried the Doctor. "What's the matter with the dog? Is he *smelling* in his sleep—as well as talking?"

"I suppose he is," said Dab-Dab. "All dogs can smell in their sleep."

"But what is he smelling?" asked the Doctor. "There is no roast beef cooking on our ship."

"No," said Dab-Dab. "The roast beef must be on that other ship over there."

"But that's ten miles away," said the Doctor. "He couldn't smell that far, surely!"

"Oh, yes, he could," said Dab-Dab. "Ask him."

Then Jip, still fast asleep, began to growl again and his lip curled up angrily, showing his clean, white teeth.

"I smell bad men," he growled, "the worst men I ever smelled. I smell trouble. I smell six bad men fighting against one brave man. I want to help him. Woof—oo—WOOF!" Then he barked and woke himself up with a surprised look on his face.

"See!" cried Dab-Dab. "That boat is nearer now. You can count its three big sails—all red. Whoever it is, they are coming after us…"

"They are bad sailors," said Jip, "and their ship is swift. They are surely the pirates of Barbary."

"Well, we must put up more sails," said the Doctor, "so we can go faster and get away from them. Run downstairs, Jip, and fetch me all the sails you see."

But even when more sails were put up on the masts, the boat did not go as fast as the pirate ship. It kept getting closer and closer.

Then the Doctor asked Dab-Dab to fly up and tell the swallows that pirates were coming after them, and ask what he should do about it.

When the swallows heard this, they all came down onto the Doctor's ship. They told him to unravel some long rope and make it into a lot of thin strings as quickly as he could. Then the ends of these strings were tied onto the front of the ship. And the swallows took hold of the strings with their feet and flew off, pulling the boat along.

And there, tied to the Doctor's ship, were a thousand strings, and two thousand swallows were pulling on each string.

They were very swift fliers! In a moment the Doctor found himself traveling so fast he had to hold his hat on with both hands.

All the animals on the ship began to laugh and dance about in the rushing air. For when they looked back at the pirate ship they could see that it was growing smaller. The red sails were being left far, far behind.

# CHAPTER TWELVE

# The Rats' Warning

Dragging a ship through the sea is hard work. After two or three hours the swallows began to get tired in the wings and short of breath. Then they sent a message down to the Doctor to say that they would pull the boat over to an island not far off to take a rest.

And soon the Doctor saw the island they had spoken of. It had a very beautiful, high, green mountain in the middle of it.

When the ship had sailed safely into the bay, the Doctor said he would get off onto the island to look for fresh water. He told all the animals to get out, too, and romp on the grass to stretch their legs.

Now, as they were getting off, the Doctor noticed that a whole lot of rats were coming up from downstairs and leaving the ship as well. Jip started to run after them, because chasing rats was his favorite game. But the Doctor told him to stop.

And one big black rat now crept forward along the rail, watching the dog out of the corner of his eye. The rat cleaned his whiskers, wiped his mouth and said, "Ahem—er—you know of course that all ships have rats in them, Doctor, do you not?"

And the Doctor said, "Yes."

"And you have heard that rats always leave a sinking ship?"

"Yes," said the Doctor, "so I've been told."

"Well," said the rat, "I've come to tell you that we are leaving this one. But we wanted to warn you before we go. This ship is not safe. The sides aren't strong enough. Its boards are rotten. It will sink to the bottom of the sea before tomorrow night."

"But how do you know?" asked the Doctor.

"We always know," answered the rat. "The tips of our tails get that tingly feeling—like when your foot's asleep. This morning, at six o'clock, while I was getting breakfast, my tail suddenly began to tingle. Then I knew, for sure, that this boat was going to sink in less than two days. It's a bad ship, Doctor. Don't sail in it any more, or you'll be surely drowned... Good-bye! We are now going to look for a good place to live on this island."

"Good-bye!" said the Doctor. "And thank you very much for coming to tell me. Very thoughtful of you—very! Leave that rat alone, Jip! Come here! Lie down!"

So then the Doctor and all his animals went off. They carried pails and saucepans to look for water on the island. The swallows took their rest.

"I wonder what is the name of this island," said the Doctor, as he was climbing up the mountain-side. "It seems a pleasant place. What a lot of birds there are!"

"Why, these are the Canary Islands," said Dab-Dab. "Don't you hear the canaries singing?"

The Doctor stopped and listened.

"Why, to be sure—of course!" he said. "I wonder if they can tell us where to find water."

Now, the canaries had heard all about Doctor Dolittle from other birds. So several canaries led him to a beautiful spring of cool, clear water where the canaries would take their baths. They showed him lovely meadows where the birdseed grew and all the other sights of their island.

And the pushmi-pullyu was glad they had come. He liked the green grass so much better than the dried apples he had been eating on the ship. And Gub-Gub squeaked for joy when he found a whole valley full of wild sugar cane.

Soon they had all had plenty to eat and drink, and were lying on their backs while the canaries sang for them. Then two of the swallows came hurrying up, very flustered and excited.

"Doctor!" they cried. "The pirates have come into the bay, and they've all got onto your ship. They are downstairs looking for things to steal. They have left their own ship with nobody on it. If you hurry and come down to the shore, you can get onto *their* ship. Their ship is very fast and you can escape in it. But you'll have to hurry."

"That's a good idea," said the Doctor. "Splendid!"

And he called his animals together at once, said good-bye to the canaries, and ran down to the beach.

When they reached the shore they saw the pirate ship, with the three red sails, standing in the water. Just as the swallows had said, there was nobody on it. All the pirates were downstairs in the Doctor's ship, looking for things to steal.

So John Dolittle told his animals to walk very softly and they all crept onto the pirate ship.

# CHAPTER THIRTEEN

# The Barbary Dragon

Everything would have gone all right if the pig had not caught a cold while eating the damp sugar cane on the island. This is what happened:

They pulled up the anchor without a sound, and were moving the pirate ship very, very carefully out of the bay. Gub-Gub suddenly sneezed so loud that the pirates on the other ship came rushing upstairs to see what the noise was.

The pirates sailed the other ship right across the entrance to the bay so that the Doctor could not get out into the open sea. Then the leader of these bad men (who called himself "Ben Ali, The Barbary Dragon") shook his fist at the Doctor.

"Ha! Ha!" he shouted. "You are caught, my fine friend! You were going to run off in my ship, eh? But you are not a good enough sailor to beat Ben Ali, the Barbary Dragon. I want that duck you've got— and the pig, too. We'll have porkchops and roast duck for supper tonight. And before I let you go home, you must make your friends send me a trunk full of gold."

Poor Gub-Gub began to weep, and Dab-Dab made ready to fly to save her life.

"Oh, let them come on," said Jip. "We can fight the dirty rascals. There are only six of them. Let them come on. I'd love to tell that collie next door, when we get home, that I had bitten a real pirate. Let 'em come. We can fight them."

"But they have pistols and swords," said the Doctor. "No, that would never do. I must talk to him… Look here, Ben Ali—"

But before the Doctor could say any more, the pirates began to sail the ship nearer. They were laughing with glee, and saying, "Who shall be the first to catch the pig?"

Poor Gub-Gub was very frightened. The pushmi-pullyu began to sharpen his horns for a fight by rubbing them on the mast of the ship. Jip kept springing into the air and barking and calling Ben Ali bad names in dog language.

But then something seemed to go wrong with the pirates. They stopped laughing and cracking jokes. They looked puzzled.

Then Ben Ali stared down at his feet and suddenly yelled out, "Thunder and lightning! Men, *the boat's leaking*!"

The other pirates peered over the side and saw that the boat was indeed getting lower and lower in the water. And one of them said to Ben Ali, "But surely if this old boat were sinking we should see the rats leaving it."

And Jip shouted across from the other ship, "You great duffers, there are no rats there to leave! They left two hours ago! Ha! Ha! to *you*!"

But of course the men did not understand him. Soon the front end of the ship began to go down and down, faster and faster. The pirates clung to the rails and masts and ropes to keep from sliding off. Then the sea rushed in through all the windows and the doors. And at last the ship plunged right down to the bottom of the sea, making a dreadful gurgling sound. And the six bad men were left bobbing about in the deep water of the bay.

# THE STORY OF
# DOCTOR DOLITTLE

Some of them started to swim for the island. Others tried to get onto the boat where the Doctor was. But Jip kept snapping at their noses, so they were afraid to climb up the side of the ship.

Then suddenly they all cried out in great fear, "*The sharks!* The sharks are coming! Let us get onto the ship before they eat us! Help, help!—The sharks! The sharks!"

All over the bay, big sharks were swimming swiftly through the water. And one great shark came near to the ship. He poked his nose out of the water and said to the Doctor, "Are you John Dolittle, the famous animal doctor?"

"Yes," said Doctor Dolittle. "That is my name."

"Well," said the shark, "we know these pirates to be a bad lot—especially Ben Ali. If they are annoying you, we will gladly eat them up for you. Then you won't be troubled any more."

"Thank you," said the Doctor. "But I don't think you need to eat them. Don't let any of them reach the shore until I tell you. Just keep them swimming about, will you? And please make Ben Ali swim over here that I may talk to him."

So the shark went off and chased Ben Ali over to the Doctor.

"Listen, Ben Ali," said John Dolittle, leaning over the side. "You have been a very bad man. These good sharks here have just offered to eat you up for me. But if you will promise to do as I tell you, I will let you go in safety."

"What must I do?" asked the pirate. He looked down sideways at the big shark who was smelling his leg under the water.

"You must kill no more people," said the Doctor. "You must stop stealing. You must never sink another ship. You must give up being a pirate altogether."

"But what shall I do then?" asked Ben Ali. "How shall I live?"

"You and all your men must go onto this island and be birdseed farmers," the Doctor answered. "You must grow birdseed for the canaries."

The Barbary Dragon turned pale with anger. "*Grow birdseed!*" he groaned in disgust. "Can't I be a sailor?"

"No," said the Doctor, "you cannot. You have been a sailor long enough—and not a very nice one. For the rest of your life you must be a peaceful farmer. The shark is waiting. Do not waste any more of his time. Make up your mind."

"Thunder and lightning!" Ben Ali muttered. "*Birdseed!*"

The big shark was then smelling his other leg.

"Very well," said the Barbary Dragon sadly. "We'll be farmers."

"And remember," said the Doctor, "that if you do not keep your promise, the canaries will come and tell me. And be very sure that I will find a way to punish you. As long as the birds and the animals and the fishes are my friends, I do not have to be afraid of a pirate chief—even though he calls himself 'The Dragon of Barbary.' Now go and be a good farmer and live in peace."

Then the Doctor turned to the big shark. He waved his hand and said, "All right. Let them swim safely to the land."

# CHAPTER FOURTEEN

## Too-Too, the Listener

The Doctor thanked the sharks for their kindness. Then he and his pets set off once more on their journey home in the swift ship with the three red sails.

As they moved out into the open sea, the animals all went downstairs to see what their new boat was like inside.

The Doctor leaned on the rail and smiled. He wondered how the monkeys were getting on and what his garden would look like when he got back to Puddleby.

Then Dab-Dab came tumbling up the stairs, all smiles and full of news.

"Doctor!" she cried. "This ship of the pirates is simply beautiful. The beds downstairs have hundreds of big silk pillows. There are thick, soft carpets on the floors. The dishes are made of silver, and there are all sorts of good things to eat and drink—special things! Just think—they kept five different kinds of cheeses, those men! Come and look… Oh, and we found a little room down there with the door locked. We are all crazy to get in and see what's inside. Jip says it must be where the pirates kept their treasure. But we can't open the door. Come down and see if you can let us in."

So the Doctor went downstairs. He found the animals gathered around a little door, all talking at once, trying to guess what was inside. The Doctor turned the handle but it wouldn't open. Jip peered through the keyhole but he could see nothing.

While they were standing around wondering what to do, the owl, Too-Too, suddenly said, "Sh! Listen! I do believe there's someone in there!"

They all kept still a moment. Then the Doctor said, "Are you sure, Too-Too? I don't hear anything."

"I'm sure of it," said the owl. "Sh!—There it is again! Don't you hear that?"

"No, I do not. What kind of a sound is it?"

"I hear the noise of someone putting his hand in his pocket," said the owl.

"But that makes hardly any sound at all," said the Doctor. "You couldn't hear that out here."

"Pardon me, but I can," said Too-Too. "I tell you there is someone on the other side of that door putting his hand in his pocket. Almost everything makes *some* noise—if your ears are only sharp enough to catch it. Bats can hear a mole walking in his tunnel under the earth. But we owls can tell you, using only one ear, the color of a kitten from the way it winks in the dark."

"Well, well!" said the Doctor. "You surprise me. That's very interesting… Listen again and tell me what he's doing now."

"I'm not sure yet," said Too-Too, "if it's a man at all. Maybe it's a woman. Lift me up and let me listen at the keyhole."

So the Doctor lifted the owl up and held him close to the lock of the door.

After a moment Too-Too said, "Now he's rubbing his face with his left hand. It is a small hand and a small face. It *might* be a woman—No. Now he pushes his hair back off his forehead—It's a man all right."

"Women sometimes do that," said the Doctor.

"True," said the owl. "But when they do, their long hair makes quite a different sound. ... Sh! Everybody be quite still. Shut your eyes and don't breathe."

Too-Too leaned down and listened again very hard and long.

At last he looked up into the Doctor's face and said, "The man in there is unhappy. He weeps. He is trying not to sniffle. But I *did* hear the sound of a tear falling on his sleeve."

"How do you know it wasn't a drop of water falling off the ceiling on him?" asked Gub-Gub.

"Pshaw! How silly," sniffed Too-Too. "A drop of water falling off the ceiling would have made ten times as much noise!"

"Well," said the Doctor, "if the poor fellow's unhappy, we've got to get in and see what's the matter with him. Find me an axe, and I'll chop the door down."

Right away an axe was found. And the Doctor soon chopped a hole in the door.

At first he could see nothing at all, it was so dark inside. So he struck a match.

The room was quite small. For furniture there was only one little stool. All round the room big barrels stood against the walls. And above the barrels, pewter jugs of all sizes hung from wooden pegs. And in the middle of the floor sat a little boy, about eight years old, crying.

"I declare, it's just a young lad!" said Jip in a whisper.

The little boy seemed rather frightened to find a man standing there and all those animals staring in through the hole of the broken door. But as soon as he saw John Dolittle's face by the light of the match, he stopped crying and got up.

"You aren't one of the pirates, are you?" the boy asked.

At that, the Doctor threw back his head and laughed long and loud. The little boy smiled, too, and came and took his hand.

"You laugh like a friend," he said, "not like a pirate. Could you tell me where my uncle is?"

"I am afraid I can't," said the Doctor. "When did you see him last?"

"It was the day before yesterday," said the boy. "My uncle and I were out fishing in our little boat, when the pirates came and caught us. They sunk

our fishing boat and brought us both onto this ship. They told my uncle that they wanted him to be a pirate like them. But he said he didn't want to be a pirate. Then the leader, Ben Ali, got very angry and gnashed his teeth, and said they would throw my uncle into the sea if he didn't do as they said. They sent me downstairs, and I heard the noise of a fight going on above. And when they let me come up again the next day, my uncle was nowhere to be seen. I asked the pirates where he was, but they wouldn't tell me. I am very much afraid they threw him into the sea and drowned him."

And the little boy began to cry again.

"Well, now—wait a minute," said the Doctor. "Don't cry. Let's go and have tea in the dining room, and we'll talk it over. Maybe your uncle is quite safe. You don't *know* that he was drowned, do you? And that's something. Perhaps we can find him for you. First we'll go and have tea with bread and strawberry jam. Then we will see what can be done."

# CHAPTER FIFTEEN

# Searches and Smells

All the animals had been standing around listening. And when they had gone into the ship's dining room and were having tea, Dab-Dab came up behind the Doctor's chair and whispered.

"Ask the porpoises if the boy's uncle was drowned—they'll know."

"All right," said the Doctor, taking a second piece of bread and jam.

"What are those funny, clicking noises you are making with your tongue?" asked the boy.

"Oh, I just said a couple of words in duck language," the Doctor answered. "This is Dab-Dab, one of my pets."

"I didn't even know that ducks had a language," said the boy. "Are all these other animals your pets, too? What is that strange-looking thing with two heads?"

"Sh!" the Doctor whispered. "That is the pushmi-pullyu. Don't let him see we're talking about him—he gets so embarrassed."

"Do you think you will be able to find my uncle for me?" asked the young boy.

"Well, we are going to try very hard," said the Doctor. "Now, what was your uncle like to look at?"

"He had red hair," the boy answered. "Very red hair. And the picture of an anchor tattooed on his arm. He was a strong man, a kind uncle, and the best sailor in the South Atlantic. His fishing boat was called *The Saucy Sally*—a cutter-rigged sloop."

"What's 'cutterigsloop'?" whispered Gub-Gub, turning to Jip.

"Sh!—That's the kind of a ship the man had," said Jip. "Keep still, can't you?"

"Oh," said the pig, "is that all? I thought it was something to drink."

So the Doctor left the boy to play with the animals in the dining room, and went upstairs to look for passing porpoises.

And soon a whole school came dancing and jumping through the water on their way to Brazil. When they saw the Doctor leaning on the rail of his ship, they came over to see how he was getting on.

And the Doctor asked them if they had seen anything of a man with red hair and an anchor tattooed on his arm.

"Do you mean the master of *The Saucy Sally*?" asked the porpoises.

"Yes," said the Doctor. "That's the man. Has he been drowned?"

"His fishing sloop was sunk," said the porpoises, "—for we saw it lying on the bottom of the sea. But there was nobody inside it, because we went and looked."

"His little nephew is on the ship with me here," said the Doctor. "He is quite afraid his uncle has drowned."

"Oh, he isn't drowned," said the porpoises. "If he were, we would have heard of it from the shrimp. We hear all the saltwater news. The shellfish call us 'The Ocean Gossips.' No—tell the little boy we are sorry we do not know where his uncle is, but we are quite certain he hasn't been drowned in the sea."

So the Doctor ran downstairs with the news and told the nephew, who clapped his hands with happiness. And the pushmi-pullyu took the little boy on his back and gave him a ride around the dining room table while all the other animals followed behind, beating the dish covers with spoons, pretending it was a parade.

"Your uncle must now be found," said the Doctor. "That is the next thing—now that we know he wasn't thrown into the sea."

Then Dab-Dab came up to him again and whispered, "Ask the eagles to look for the man. No living creature can see better than an eagle. When they are miles high in the air they can count the ants crawling on the ground. Ask the eagles."

So the Doctor sent one of the swallows off to get some eagles. And in about an hour the little bird came back with six different kinds of eagles: a Black Eagle, a Bald Eagle, a Fish Eagle, a Golden Eagle, an Eagle-Vulture, and a White-tailed Sea Eagle. And they stood on the rail of the ship, like round-shouldered soldiers all in a row, stern and still and stiff. Their great, gleaming, black eyes shot darting glances here and there and everywhere.

Gub-Gub was scared and got behind a barrel.

The Doctor said to the eagles, "This boy's uncle has been lost—a fisherman with red hair and an anchor marked on his arm. Would you be so kind as to see if you can find him for us?"

Eagles do not talk very much. All they answered in their husky voices was, "You may be sure that we will do our best for John Dolittle."

Then they flew off—and Gub-Gub came out from behind his barrel to see them go. Up and up and up they went—higher and higher and higher. Then they flew in different directions—North, East, South, and West, looking like tiny grains of black sand creeping across the wide, blue sky.

"My gracious!" said Gub-Gub in a hushed voice. "They are so near the sun! I hope they don't burn their feathers!"

They were gone a long time. And when they came back it was almost night.

And the eagles said to the Doctor, "We have searched all the seas and all the countries and all the islands and all the cities and all the villages in this half of the world. But we have failed. Nowhere could we see any sign of this boy's uncle. And if we could not see him, then he is not to be seen. For John Dolittle, we have done our best."

Then the six great birds flapped their big wings and flew back to their homes in the mountains and the rocks.

"Well," said Dab-Dab, "what are we going to do now? The boy's uncle *must* be found. I wish Chee-Chee were here. He would soon find the man. Good old Chee-Chee! I wonder how he's getting on!"

"If we only had Polynesia with us," said the white mouse, "*she* would soon think of some way. Do you remember how she got us all out of prison—the second time? My, but she was a clever one!"

"I don't think so much of those eagle fellows," said Jip. "They're just stuck up. They may have very good eyesight, but when you ask them to find a man for you, they can't do it. And they have the nerve to say that nobody else could do it. And I don't think a whole lot of those gossipy old porpoises either. All they could tell us was that the man isn't in the sea. We don't want to know where he *isn't*—we want to know where he *is*."

"It's easy to grumble," said Gub-Gub, "but it isn't so easy to find a man when you have to hunt the whole world for him. You couldn't find the boy's uncle any more than the eagles could."

"Couldn't I?" said the dog. "That's what you think, you silly little piglet! I haven't begun to try yet, have I? You wait and see!"

Then Jip went to the Doctor and said, "Please ask the boy if he has anything in his pockets that belonged to his uncle."

So the Doctor asked him. The boy took from his pocket a great big red handkerchief and said, "This was my uncle's."

As soon as the boy pulled it out, Jip shouted, "*Peppermint*, by Jingo! Richard's Oil of Peppermint tablets. Don't you smell it? Your uncle takes peppermints, doesn't he?"

"Yes. My uncle took a lot of peppermints—for his stomach."

"Fine!" said Jip. "The man's as good as found. It will be as easy as stealing milk from a kitten. Tell the boy I'll find his uncle for him in less than a week. Let us go upstairs and see which way the wind is blowing."

As they climbed the stairs, Jip explained, "Wind is very important in long-distance smelling. It mustn't be a fierce wind. And of course it must blow the right way. A nice, steady breeze is the best of all… Ha! This wind is from the North."

Then Jip went up to the front of the ship and smelled the wind. He started muttering to himself, "Tar. Spanish onions. Lamp oil. Wet raincoats. Crushed leaves. Lace curtains being washed—no, my mistake, lace curtains hanging out to dry. And foxes—hundreds of 'em—cubs. And—"

"Can you really smell all those different things in this one wind?" asked the Doctor.

"Why, of course!" said Jip. "Those are only a few of the easy smells. Wait now, and I'll tell you some of the harder scents that are coming on this wind."

Then the dog shut his eyes tight, poked his nose straight up in the air and sniffed hard, his mouth half-open. For a long time he said nothing. He kept as still as a stone. He hardly seemed to breathe at all. When at last he began to speak, it sounded almost as if he were singing sadly in a dream.

"Bricks," he whispered, very low, "old yellow bricks, crumbling with age in a garden wall. The sweet breath of young cows standing in a mountain stream. The tin roof of a henhouse with the midday sun on it. A dusty road with sycamore trees. Little mushrooms bursting through rotting leaves. And—and—and—"

"Any parsnips?" asked Gub-Gub.

"No," said Jip. "You always think of things to eat. No parsnips. And no peppermint. Plenty of sugar candies and sweet cream, and a few chocolates. But no peppermint. We must wait till the wind changes to the South."

"I think you're a fake, Jip," said Gub-Gub. "Who ever heard of finding a man in the middle of the ocean just by smell! I knew you couldn't do it."

"Look here," said Jip, getting really angry. "You're going to get a bite on the nose in a minute!"

"Stop quarreling!" said the Doctor. "Stop it! Life's too short. Tell me, Jip, where do you think those smells are coming from?"

"From Devon and Wales, most of them," said Jip. "The wind is coming that way."

"Well, well!" said the Doctor. "You know that's really quite remarkable. I must make a note of that for my new book. I wonder if you could train me to smell as well as that. … But no—perhaps I'm better off the way I am. Let's go down to supper. I'm quite hungry."

"So am I," said Gub-Gub.

# CHAPTER SIXTEEN

## The Rock

Up they got early next morning. The sun was shining brightly and the wind was blowing from the South. Jip smelled the wind for half an hour.

"I smell no peppermint," he said. "We must wait till the wind changes to the East."

But even when the East wind came, at three o'clock that afternoon, the dog could not catch the smell of peppermint. The little boy was very sad at this and began to cry again. But all Jip said to the Doctor was, "Tell him that when the wind changes to the West, I'll find his uncle. I'll find him even if he's in China—as long as he still has the Richard's Oil of Peppermint tablets with him."

Three days they had to wait before the West wind came. This was on a Friday morning, early. As soon as Jip awoke he ran upstairs and poked his nose in the air. Then he got excited and rushed down again to wake the Doctor up.

"Doctor!" he cried. "I've got it! Doctor! Doctor! Wake up! Listen! I've got it! The wind's from the West and it smells of nothing but peppermint. Come upstairs and start the ship—quick!"

So the Doctor tumbled out of bed and went to the rudder to steer the ship.

"Now, I'll go up to the front," said Jip, "and you watch my nose. Whichever way I point it, you turn the ship the same way. The man cannot be far off, with the smell as strong as this. Now watch me!"

So all that morning Jip stood in the front part of the ship, sniffing the wind and pointing the way for the Doctor to steer. All the animals and the little boy stood around with their eyes wide open, watching the dog in wonder.

About lunchtime Jip spoke to the Doctor in private. "The boy's uncle is starving," he said. "We must make the ship go as fast as we can."

"How do you know he is starving?" asked the Doctor.

"Because there is no other smell in the West wind but peppermint," said Jip. "If the man were cooking or eating food of any kind, I would smell it, too. But he hasn't even fresh water to drink. All he is taking is peppermint tablets. We are getting nearer all the time, for the smell grows stronger every minute. But make the ship go as fast as you can, for I am certain that the man is starving."

"All right," said the Doctor. He sent Dab-Dab to ask the swallows to pull the ship, the same as they had done when the pirates were chasing them.

So the stout little birds came down and once more began to pull the ship. And now the boat went speeding through the sea. It went so fast that the fishes had to jump for their lives to get out of the way and not be run over.

All the animals got very excited. They watched the sea in front for any land or islands where the starving man might be. But hour after hour went by and still the ship went rushing on, over the same flat, flat sea. No land came in sight.

And now the animals sat around silent. The little boy again grew sad. And on Jip's face there was a worried look. It was already late in the afternoon and the sun was going down.

Suddenly, the owl, Too-Too, who was perched on the tip of the mast, cried out, "Jip! Jip! I see a great, great rock in front of us! Look! See the sun shine on it? Is the smell coming from there?"

And Jip called back, "Yes. That's it. That is where the man is. At last, at last!"

And when they got nearer they could see that the rock was very large. No trees grew on it, no grass—nothing. The great rock was as smooth and as bare as the back of a tortoise.

Then the Doctor sailed the ship all the way around the rock. All the animals squinted their eyes and looked as hard as they could. John Dolittle got a telescope from downstairs.

But not one living thing could they spy—not even a gull, nor a starfish, nor a shred of seaweed.

They all stood still and listened. But the only noise they heard was the gentle lapping of the little waves against the sides of their ship.

Then they all started calling, "Hulloa, there! HULLOA!" till their voices were hoarse. But only the echo came back from the rock.

The little boy burst into tears and said, "I am afraid I shall never see my uncle anymore!"

But Jip called to the Doctor, "He must be there—he must—*he must*! The smell stops here. He must be there, I tell you! Sail the ship close to the rock and let me jump out on it."

So the Doctor brought the ship as close as he could and let down the anchor. Then he and Jip got out of the ship and onto the rock.

Jip at once put his nose down close to the ground and began to run all over the place. Up and down he went, back and forth.

At last Jip let out a great bark and sat down. And when the Doctor came running up to him, he found the dog staring into a big, deep hole in the middle of the rock.

"The boy's uncle is down there," said Jip quietly. "No wonder those silly eagles couldn't see him! It takes a dog to find a man."

So the Doctor got down into the hole, which seemed to be a kind of cave. Then he struck matches and made his way along a very long, dark tunnel with Jip following behind.

At last the tunnel came to an end, and the Doctor found himself in a kind of tiny room with walls of rock.

And there, in the middle of the room, his head resting on his arms, lay a man with very red hair—fast asleep!

Jip went up and sniffed at something lying on the ground beside him. The Doctor stooped and picked it up. It was a rather large tin. And inside were Richard's Oil of Peppermint tablets!

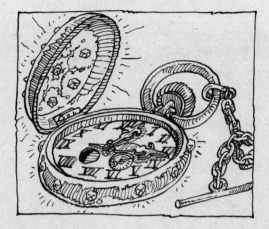

# CHAPTER SEVENTEEN

# The Fisherman's Town

Gently then—very gently—the Doctor woke the man up.

But just at that moment the match went out. The man thought it was Ben Ali, the Barbary Dragon, coming back, and he began to punch at the Doctor in the dark.

But when John Dolittle told him who it was, and that he had his little nephew safe on his ship, the man was tremendously glad. He said he was sorry he had punched at the Doctor. He had not hurt him much, though, because it was too dark to punch properly.

Then he gave the Doctor a peppermint.

And the man told how the Barbary Dragon had put him onto this rock and left him there when he wouldn't promise to become a pirate. He had slept down in the hole because there was no house on the rock to keep him warm.

And then he said, "For four days I have had nothing to eat or drink. I have lived on peppermints."

"There you are!" said Jip. "What did I tell you?"

So they struck some more matches and made their way out through the tunnel into the daylight. Then the Doctor hurried the man down to the boat to get some soup.

When the animals and the little boy saw the Doctor and Jip coming back to the ship with a red-headed man, they began to cheer and yell and dance about the boat. And the swallows up above started whistling at the top of their voices. The noise they made was so great that sailors far out at sea thought that a terrible storm was coming. "Hark to that wind howling in the East!" they said.

And Jip was awfully proud of himself, though he tried hard not to look stuck-up. When Dab-Dab came to him and said, "Jip, I had no idea you were so clever!" he just tossed his head and answered,

"Oh, that's nothing special. But it takes a dog to find a man, you know. Birds are no good for a game like that."

Then the Doctor asked the red-haired fisherman where his home was. And when he had told him, the Doctor asked the swallows to guide the ship there first.

They came at last to the fisherman's land. There they saw a little fishing town at the foot of a rocky mountain. The man pointed out the house where he lived.

And while they were letting down the anchor, the little boy's mother (who was also the man's sister) came running down to the shore to meet them, laughing and crying at the same time. She had been sitting on a hill for twenty days, watching the sea and waiting for them to return.

And she kissed the Doctor many times, so that he giggled and blushed. And she tried to kiss Jip, too, but he ran away and hid inside the ship.

The fisherman and his sister didn't want the Doctor to go away again in a hurry. They begged him to spend a few days with them. So John Dolittle and his animals had to stay at their house a whole Saturday and Sunday and half of Monday.

# THE STORY OF DOCTOR DOLITTLE

And all the little boys of the fishing village went down to the beach and pointed at the great ship. They said to one another in whispers, "Look! That was a pirate ship—Ben Ali's, the most terrible pirate that ever sailed the Seven Seas! That old gentleman with the high hat, he took the ship away from The Barbary Dragon. He made that pirate into a birdseed farmer. … Look at the great red sails! Ain't she a grand ship—and fast?—My!"

All this time in the little fishing town, the people kept asking him out to teas and dinners and parties. All the ladies sent him boxes of flowers and candies. And the village band played tunes under his window every night.

At last the Doctor said, "Good people, I must go home now. You have really been most kind. I shall always remember it. But I must go home, for I have things to do."

Then, just as the Doctor was about to leave, the Mayor of the Town came down the street and a lot of other people in grand clothes with him. The Mayor stopped before the house where the Doctor was staying. Everybody in the village gathered around to see what was going to happen.

Six boys blew on shining trumpets to make the people stop talking. Then the Doctor came out onto the steps.

And the Mayor said, "Doctor John Dolittle, it is a great pleasure for me to present to the man who rid the seas of the Dragon of Barbary this little token from the grateful people of our town."

The Mayor opened a tissue-paper packet and handed to the Doctor a beautiful watch with real diamonds in the back.

Then the Mayor pulled something else from his pocket. "Where is the dog?" he said.

Then everybody started to hunt for Jip. And at last Dab-Dab found him on the other side of the village in the stable yard. There, all the dogs of the countryside were standing around him speechless, with great respect.

Jip was brought to the Doctor's side. A great murmur of wonder went up from the village folk as the Mayor bent down and fastened a dog collar made of solid gold around Jip's neck. Written on the collar in big letters were these words:

JIP—The Cleverest Dog in the World.

Then the whole crowd moved down to the beach to see them off. The red-haired fisherman and his sister and the little boy had thanked the Doctor and his dog over and over and over again. Then the great, swift ship with the red sails was turned once more toward Puddleby and they sailed out to sea, while the village band played music on the shore.

# CHAPTER EIGHTEEN

# Home Again

March winds had come and gone. April's showers were over. May's buds had opened into flower. And the June sun was shining on the pleasant fields when John Dolittle at last got back to his own country.

But he did not yet go home to Puddleby. First he went traveling through the land with the pushmi-pullyu in a gypsy wagon. He stopped at all the country fairs and set up his wagon. Then he hung out a big sign that read:

COME & SEE THE TWO-HEADED ANIMAL
FROM THE JUNGLES OF AFRICA.
Admission: SIXPENCE

COME & SEE
THE
TWO-HEADED
ANIMAL
FROM THE JUNGLES
OF AFRICA
ADMISSION
6D.

And the pushmi-pullyu would stay inside the wagon, while the other animals would lie about underneath. The Doctor sat in a chair in front taking the sixpences and smiling at the people as they went in. Dab-Dab often scolded him for letting the children in for free.

And zoo keepers and circus men came and asked the Doctor to sell them the strange creature. But the Doctor always shook his head and said, "No. The pushmi-pullyu shall never be shut up in a cage. He shall be free always to come and go, like you and me."

So many people came flocking to the little wagon to see the pushmi-pullyu that very soon the Doctor was quite rich and was able to give up being a showman. This was good, for they were all longing to go home.

And one fine day, when the hollyhocks were in full bloom, he came back to Puddleby to live in the little house with the big garden.

And the old lame horse in the stable was glad to see him. And Dab-Dab was glad, too, to get back to the house she knew so well—although there was such a lot of dusting to be done, with cobwebs everywhere.

And after Jip had gone and shown his golden collar to the collie next door, he came back and began running round the garden. He went looking for the bones he had buried long ago, and chasing the rats out of the tool shed. And Gub-Gub dug up the horseradish which had grown three feet high in the corner by the garden wall.

The Doctor went and saw the sailor who had lent him the boat, and he bought two new ships for him and a rubber doll for his baby. Then he paid the food store man for the food he had lent him for the journey to Africa. And he bought another piano and put the white mice back in it.

The Doctor filled the old money box on the dresser shelf. And he *still* had money left. He had to get three more money boxes to put the rest in.

"Money," he said, "is a terrible nuisance. But it's nice not to have to worry."

"Yes," said Dab-Dab, who was toasting muffins for his tea, "it is indeed!"

And when the Winter came again, and the snow flew against the kitchen window, the Doctor and his animals would sit round the big, warm fire after supper. And he would read aloud to them out of his books.

# THE STORY OF
# DOCTOR DOLITTLE

But far away in Africa, where the monkeys chattered in the palm trees before they went to bed under the big yellow moon, they would say to one another, "I wonder what the Good Doctor's doing now, over there in the Land of England! Do you think he ever will come back?"

And Polynesia would squeak out from the vines, "I think he will—I guess he will—I hope he will!"

And then the crocodile would grunt up at them from the black mud of the river, "I'm *sure* he will. Go to sleep!"

## THE END

# HUGH LOFTING

Hugh Lofting was born in Maidenhead, England, in 1886, and was home-schooled until he was eight. He went to college in England and Massachusetts, and he became an American citizen in 1919.

During the Great War (WWI), Lofting served in the Irish Guard. When he wrote letters home to his children, he drew pictures for them. He told them how important the animals were in the war effort—how they pulled equipment, how they gave some comfort at times. The letters led him to write about a kind, thoughtful country doctor who cares about animals and the natural world.

*The Story of Doctor Dolittle* was published in 1920, introducing children all over the world to this clever, peaceful Doctor who learns animal languages so that he can care for his animal patients. Lofting's next book, *The Voyages of Doctor Dolittle* (1922), was awarded the Newbery Medal in 1923. The witty words, the characters, and the adventures delight children. The Doctor's respect for the world and all living things delights readers of every age and every era.

Hugh Lofting wrote many more books about Doctor Dolittle and his adventures. Lofting died at his home in California in 1947.